JACK RUSSELL:
Dog Detective

The Kitnapped Creature

DARREL & SALLY ODGERS

SCHOLASTIC INC.

New York   Toronto   London   Auckland   Sydney
Mexico City   New Delhi   Hong Kong   Buenos Aires

ISBN-13: 978-0-545-03338-1
ISBN-10: 0-545-03338-1

First published by Scholastic Press in 2007.
Text copyright © 2007 by Sally and Darrel Odgers.
Cover design copyright © 2007 by Lake Shore Graphics.
Dog, Frisbee, courtesy of the Cansick family.
Interior illustrations by Janine Dawson.
Interior illustrations copyright © 2007 Scholastic Australia.

12 11 10 9 8 7 6 5 4 3   8 9 10 11 12 13/0

Printed in the U.S.A.
First Scholastic printing, February 2008

Dear Readers,

The story you're about to read is about me and my friends, and how we solved the Case of the Kitnapped Creature. To save time, I'll introduce us all to you now. Of course, if you know us already, you can trot off to Chapter One.

I am Jack Russell, Dog Detective. I live with my landlord, Sarge, in Doggeroo. Sarge detects human-type crimes. I have the important job of detecting crimes that deal with dogs. I'm a Jack Russell terrier, so I am dogged and intelligent. Preacher lives with us. He is a clever, handsome, junior Jack Russell. His mother is my friend Jill Russell.

Next door to Sarge and me live Auntie Tidge and Foxy. Auntie Tidge is lovely. She has special biscuits. Foxy is not lovely. He's a fox terrier (more or less). He used to be a street dog, and a thief, but he's reformed now. Auntie Tidge has even got rid of his fleas. Foxy sometimes helps me with my cases.

Uptown Lord Setter (Lord Red for short) lives in Uptown House with Caterina Smith. Lord Red means well, but he isn't very bright.

We have other friends in Doggeroo. These include Polly the dachshund, the squekes, Ralf Boxer, and Shuffle the pug. Then there's Fat Molly Cat from the library.

That's all you need to know, so let's get on with Chapter One.

Yours doggedly,

Jack Russell—the detective with a nose for crime

Preacher

It was past breakfast time, and my food bowl was empty.

I was about to leap out of my basket and **assess the situation** when I remembered something **pawfully** important. I was sharing my basket with someone else.

Jack's Facts

No one can force a Jack to share.
Some Jacks choose to share.
If a Jack chooses to share, that is
pawfectly *fine.*
This is a fact.

I crawled out from under my blanket and trotted down the steps into my yard.

I was doing what dogs do when I heard a squeak. Next came a whine. The whine quickly grew to a yelp, and then to a screech.

Preacher was awake.

That's my boy! I thought. I was as quiet as a Jack could be, but he detected the **Jack-gap** when I left the basket. I was proud of him.

I trotted back and stuck my nose under the blanket. The screeching stopped.

"You left me!" yipped Preacher.

"I had to do what dogs do before breakfast," I explained. "You should do it, too."

Preacher peered over the edge of the basket. "I can't get out."

"**Of paws** you can," I said.

"I can't. I can't. I—"

I pushed my nose under his fat tummy and flipped him out of the basket. "Come on," I said. "No puddles in bed."

Preacher picked himself up. "You flipped me."

I hustled Preacher down the steps. When he had made a puddle, I took him around the garden. The puppy had a lot to learn.

Jack's Facts

All dogs learn things.
Smart dogs learn more than dim dogs.
Jack Russells learn a lot.
Therefore, Jacks are the smartest dogs of all.
This is a fact.

"What are you doing, Dad?" he asked when I *sniff-sniffed* the air.

"I'm making a **nose map**. Sit, sniff, and detect."

Jack's Map

1. My basket with the blanket
   Auntie Tidge knitted.

2. My **squeaker bone**.

3. My empty food bowl.

4. Preacher's empty
   food bowl.

5. Fat Molly Cat,
   stalking a bird.

6. Preacher's **teddy bear**.

7. Foxy, skulking behind the hedge.

Preacher made a nose map, too.

Preacher's Map

1. Sleepy place.

2. Dad's toy.

3. Dad's foody.

4. My foody.

5. Ouchy-claw creature.

6. My chewy thing.

7. Snappy snarly thing.

I was proud of him, but I had to explain that Jacks don't have toys.

I sniffed the air (still no breakfast) and trotted to the hedge.

"Pssst! Foxy!"

Foxy snarled. "I'm not talking to you, Jack Russell."

I **ig-gnawed** that. "Foxy, guess what Preacher did?"

"Ruined your best pal's life?" growled Foxy.

"**Dogwash**! Guess what he did?"

"Don't know. Don't care."

"He made his very first nose map! Guess what he calls *you*?"

"Don't care," said Foxy. "I'm not talking to him."

"He calls you snappy snarly thing," I reported. I thought it was funny. Foxy didn't.

"Have you had breakfast?" I asked.

"Of paws," said Foxy. "I had beef and sausage. Then I had a **special biscuit** and a **liver treat**. Auntie Tidge promised me a whole oxtail for dinner."

The pup and I went to check our bowls, but they were still empty. Something was very wrong.

Jack's Glossary

Assess the situation. *Find out what is happening.*

Pawfully. *Very; awfully.*

Pawfectly. *Perfectly, only used for dogs.*

Jack-gap. *Gap where a noble Jack Russell was just a moment ago.*

Of paws. *Of course.*

Nose map. *Way of storing information collected by the nose.*

Squeaker bone. *Item for exercising teeth. Not to be confused with a toy.*

Teddy bear. *Item for Jack Russell pups to chew or sit on. Not a toy.*

Ig-gnawed. *Ignored, but done by dogs.*

Dogwash. *Nonsense.*

Special biscuits. *Auntie Tidge makes these. They don't harm terrier teeth.*

Liver treat. *Crunchy, delicious treat Auntie Tidge makes.*

Sarge

"We must investigate," I told Preacher.

I led the way to the **dogdoor**, and scooted through into the kitchen.

Preacher tried to follow, but the dogdoor swung back and smacked his nose. Preacher growled at the dogdoor and pushed inside. I was proud of him.

We *sniff-sniffed* the kitchen. No Sarge. No toast. No tea. No beef. No milk. We *sniff-sniffed* through the house and tracked Sarge to the bedroom. I **Jack-jumped** to paw the doorhandle.

The door swung open. Sarge was still in bed. I **Jack-yapped** to let him know this was unacceptable. Preacher **pup-yapped**. I was proud of him.

Sarge groaned. "Jack . . . help!" His hand was dangling over the edge of the bed. It felt hot. I nosed it to let him know I would fetch help immediately.

Jack's Facts

Bad people are too lazy to feed their dogs.
Good people are not.
If a good person doesn't feed his dogs, he
needs help.
This is a fact.

"Sarge is sick," I told Preacher. "Stand guard. Lick his hand."

I knew Preacher would obey, because junior Jacks always obey their **Jack-pack** leaders. I scooted out of the house, left the yard (never mind how), and galloped to the second-best person in the world.

Foxy snarled as I raced up his path. "Get out of my **terrier-tory**, Jack!"

Auntie Tidge was in the kitchen making special biscuits. I did the **paw**

thing and Jack-yapped. I bounced in and out through the dogdoor. "**Jackie Wackie**? What's wrong?" asked Auntie Tidge.

I Jack-yapped, and dashed home. Auntie Tidge is not in the right shape for running, but she followed anyway.

Preacher was still standing guard. Auntie Tidge looked at Sarge and rushed to the **terrier-phone**.

Jack's Glossary

Dogdoor. *A door especially for dogs.*

Jack-jump. *A very athletic spring done by a Jack Russell terrier.*

Jack-yap. *A loud, piercing yap made by a Jack Russell terrier.*

Pup-yap. *A loud, piercing yap made by a junior Jack Russell terrier.*

Jack-pack. *A noble pack of dogs united under a strong leader.*

Terrier-tory. *A territory owned by a terrier.*

Paw thing. *Up on hind legs, paws held together as if praying. Means pleased excitement.*

Jackie Wackie. *Auntie Tidge is the only person allowed to call me that.*

Terrier-phones. *Thing that rings.*

Ranger Jack

An ambulance took Sarge to the hospital. Auntie Tidge said the **doctors** would help him. She packed our things, then took us to her place for breakfast.

Foxy was furious. "This is *my* terrier-tory and that is *my* breakfast."

I growled back. "You already ate your breakfast."

"That's my *tomorrow's* breakfast," said Foxy.

"Foxy Woxy," said Auntie Tidge. "You be nice to Jackie Wackie and Preacher while I'm at the hospital."

Foxy grumbled. He loves Auntie

Tidge, but he didn't want to be nice to us.

When Auntie Tidge had gone, Foxy stole Preacher's teddy bear.

Preacher whined. Sarge gave him that bear. It's special.

"Ig-gnaw him, Preacher," I said. I didn't feel like breakfast now. We went home.

I was miserable without Sarge, although I tried to stay **paw-sitive** for the pup's sake. "Sarge will be back," I told him. "He would never desert us."

Every day, Auntie Tidge fed us at her place. Foxy growled or ig-gnawed us. Some dogs get pawfully **paw-sessive**.

We slept in Foxy's kitchen because Preacher was a puppy. That made Foxy angrier.

Auntie Tidge gave us liver treats and special biscuits, but Foxy said he should have them all. "That puppy must stay

away from my old boot," he said. "He can't
dig in Auntie Tidge's herb garden. I don't
want either of you in my patch of sun."

After days of Foxy being **im-paw-sible**,
I got bored. "Let's go for a walk," I said.

Foxy jumped up. "We'll chase rabbits
at the preserve. The puppy can stay here."

"I wasn't talking to you," I said.

We left Foxy's yard (never mind
how), and trotted along the street.

Preacher wanted to visit Jill Russell, but I was afraid Jill's people would think Preacher was homesick. "Let's go to Uptown House," I said. "We can play hide-and-squeak with Lord Red."

We were crossing the showgrounds when Preacher stopped. "Who's that nice person, Dad? He smells like liver treats." He *sniff-sniffed*. His tail waggled.

I used my **super-sniffer** to pinpoint the smell. It was coming from a familiar van.

"Record that smell in your **smell-bank**," I told Preacher. "That is Ranger Jack."

"He smells nice," said Preacher, sniffing and waggling.

"He is nice," I agreed. "But remember, it's Ranger Jack's job to catch stray dogs."

Preacher's tail tucked between his legs. "What if he caught me?"

"He'd put you in the pound," I said.

Preacher whined. "I don't want Ranger Jack to put me in the pound."

"It wouldn't be forever. Sarge would pay money to bail you out."

"That's all right, then," said Preacher, but then I remembered Sarge wasn't home. Neither was Auntie Tidge. If Ranger Jack caught us, who would bail us out?

And *when* was Sarge coming home?

We left the showgrounds and headed for the preserve.

Preacher was practicing nose maps when I saw him **hackle**. "I just nose-mapped an ouchie-claw creature!" he said.

I was pawfully proud of him.

"That'll be Fat Molly from the library," I said. "She's an enemy."

"Like the snappy snarly thing," said Preacher.

"Foxy's not an enemy," I said. "He's a pal."

"He doesn't act like a pal," said Preacher.

Preacher had a point, so I stopped to think about it.

Jack's Facts

If pals are sometimes snappy and snarly, they are still pals.
If pals are always snappy and snarly, they are not pals.
This is a fact.

"Let's detect the ouchie-claw creature," said Preacher.

I agreed. I thought it would amuse the pup, but instead it turned into the Case of the Kitnapped Creature.

Jack's Glossary

Doctors. *Vets for people.*

Paw-sitive. *Positive and cheerful, for dogs.*

Paw-sessive. *The way some dogs feel about their homes and belongings.*

Im-paw-sible. *Like impossible.*

Super-sniffer. *Jack's nose in super-tracking mode.*

Smell-bank. *A store of smells that must be remembered.*

Hackle. *Raising the hair on the back of the neck in fear or excitement.*

Cat-erwaul

We tracked the ouchie-claw creature through the preserve.

"It's called a cat," I told Preacher.

"Cats are scary," said the pup. "Cats scratch pups. Mom Russell said so."

"Jill Russell is clever," I said. "But most cats run if you Jack-yap. We'll play **cat-ch cat** and I'll show you."

We tracked the cat through some bushes. I was **paw-plexed**. Most cats would have detected us and made a run for it. Why did this cat **ig-claw** us?

Preacher *sniff-sniffed* hard. His tail stuck straight out.

Jack's Facts

Up-tail means a happy Jack.
Down-tail means a sad or nervous Jack.
Straight-tail means stalking mode.
Jack-tails are **im-paw-tant.**
This is a fact.

That's when we heard the sudden **cat-erwaul.** *Yeeeowww-psssst!*

"What's that?" Preacher's tail went low.

"It's a cat-erwaul," I explained. "Cats do that to unnerve dogs."

Yeeeowww-psssst! Yeeeowww-wongwongwong-psssst!

This time, the cat-erwaul was worse.

My tail dropped. Hackles rose on my neck. I snarled.

"Do we have to play cat-ch cat?" asked

Preacher. "C-can't we see Mom instead?"

Yeeeowww-psssst! Yeeeowww-wongwongwong-psssst! Prowwwssssstttt!

I stopped. Jacks are bold. Jacks are brave. Jacks are frightened of (almost) nothing. Jacks are *not* unkind. If this cat didn't want to play, we should **respect its wishes**. Besides, I had smelled this cat before . . . and it wasn't Fat Molly.

I was about to explain to Preacher when we heard something else.

Psssst!

"Ouch! I'll get you yet!"

"What's that?" asked Preacher.

"I'm not sure," I admitted.

Preacher sat down and licked his nose. "Let's make a nose map."

"Pawfect!" I was proud of him.

1. Familiar Cat.

2. Preacher.

3. Strange person with shoes
   that smell as if they need
   chewing.

4. Fish treats.

Preacher's Map

1. Ouchy-claw—um, cat.

2. Dad.

3. Yucky person.

4. Yummy!

We compared notes. I explained to Preacher that the "yummy" he had detected was a fish treat. Then we heard the caterwaul again.

Yeeeowww-psssst! Yeeeowww-wongwongwong-psssst! Prowwwssssstttt!

"Ouchhhh!"

Then came a truly **terrier-able** noise. My hackles stood up. Preacher screeched and fled. I wasn't frightened, but a Jack must do his duty. I'd promised Jill Russell I'd keep the puppy safe. I fled after him.

Jack's Glossary

Cat-ch cat. *A game dogs play with cats.*

Paw-plexed. *Perplexed and puzzled.*

Ig-claw. *Like ignore, but done by cats.*

Im-paw-tant. *Important, for dogs.*

Cat-erwaul. *A horrible noise made by a cat.*

Respect its wishes. *Stop doing whatever you're doing.*

Terrier-able. *Very bad.*

Lord Red

I had smelled that cat and heard that
cat-erwaul before. I raced as fast as
Preacher could go. My mind raced faster.
I added one to one and one and came
up with one.

Jack's Facts

*If you take one horrible familiar cat-
erwaul,
and add one familiar smell and one
yelling human,
you get one familiar monster cat.
This is a fact.*

34

The only monster cat I knew was the
Awful Pawful . . . but wasn't he far away?

Something with big paws was
chasing us. It was catching up fast.

Jack's Facts

Jacks are fast dogs.
Junior Jack pups are not as fast.
Jacks must not leave pups behind when
they are afraid.
This is a fact.

My paws wanted to go faster.
Preacher was tired. I made an **executive
decision**. It is better to stop and fight
than get caught by the tail.

"Drop!" I ordered Preacher.

Preacher dropped into a crouch like a
rabbit. I stopped and spun around. I was

ready to fight to the death to defend my
pup.

The big-pawed creature was still
coming, so I dived forward, snarling and
hackling. A Jack in a rage is a truly
terrier-fying sight.

The creature pranced toward us.
"Jack? Jack! Why are you running, Jack?
Are you playing cat-ch cat? Can I play,
too?"

It was Lord Red.

"Halt!" I said.

Red noticed Preacher. He crouched,
and poked Preacher with his nose.
"Hello, very small dog. Are you a
chihuahua like Ralf Boxer? Will you bite
my nose?"

Preacher sat up and pawed at Red's

nose. He yipped. Red went cross-eyed.

"This is Preacher," I said. "He's a junior Jack Russell."

"Does he belong to you, Jack? You are lucky! Yowp!" Preacher had nipped his nose.

I Jack-yapped for attention. "Lord Red, something terrier-able has happened. The Awful Pawful is back in Doggeroo."

Red's eyes bugged. He quivered. "The Awful Pawful! Nooooo! Hellllp!" He crouched and buried his nose in his paws. Then he peeped at me with one eye. "What's an Awful Pawful, Jack?"

"You remember," I said. "It is a huge orange cat with very sharp claws. It **terrier-ized** all the dogs in Doggeroo. They were too scared to go out."

"I remember now." He sat up. "But it's all right, Jack. Don't you remember? Ranger Jack took the Awful Pawful away in his van." Red is not the brightest biscuit in the packet.

"The Awful Pawful is back," I said. "I have to investigate, but there's a problem."

I looked at Preacher. So did Red. Preacher growled.

"I am *not* a problem! I am a Jack Russell terrier. Mom said so."

"Of paws!" I said. "You are brave and bold. *But* you are not big." I gulped. I didn't feel big, either.

"The Awful Pawful might eat you!" said Red. "Do huge, big cats eat very small dogs, Jack?"

"Let's not find out. Red, does Caterina Smith know you're out?"

"Of paws not!" said Red. "Caterina Smith doesn't like it when I leave the yard, so I do it when she—"

"Red!" I snapped. "This is your mission! Take Preacher to Foxy's place. Stay until I return."

Red whined. So did Preacher. "Foxy

hates me!" they said together.

"You can **trust** Foxy in an emergency," I said.

"Really?" Red leaped up. "Come on, very small dog," he said to Preacher. "We're going to Foxy's."

Jack's Glossary

Executive decision. *Decision made by pack leader on behalf of others.*

Terrier-fying. *Frightening.*

Terrier-ized. *Frightened.*

Trust. *More im-paw-tant than almost anything.*

Chewy Shoes

Red trotted off with Preacher. I stayed. If the Awful Pawful was back, it was my duty to investigate.

I crept toward the bushes where we had nose-mapped the Awful Pawful. I could still hear a terrier-able lot of noise. It sounded like a fight. Who'd fight the Awful Pawful?

I crawled under a bush and crept forward on my elbows. I stopped to sniff-sniff often to make sure I was on the right track.

Yeeeowww-wongwongwong!

That was the Awful Pawful. No other cat makes such a terrier-able cat-erwaul. My hackles rose. I stuck my nose out from under the bush.

There was the monster cat, but it wasn't fighting. It was in a cage.

Someone had hidden a cage in the preserve. I *sniff-sniffed.* I could smell fish treats. It was clear to me that the Awful Pawful had gone into the cage after the fish treats. Now it was trying to get out.

The cage was open. A person with chewy-looking shoes was trying to shut the door.

It was enough to make a dog laugh.

Chewy Shoes put his hand on the door. The Awful Pawful darted forward. The Awful Pawful cat-erwauled and swung a **claw-full** pawful. Chewy Shoes

swore and jumped back. This happened
over and over. Chewy Shoes had claw
marks on his hands. The Awful Pawful's
ears were so far back I could hardly see
them.

Come on, I thought to Chewy Shoes.
You can do it! I prepared for a fast
getaway in case he couldn't. In the end,

Chewy Shoes kicked the door shut.

Yeeeowww-psssst! The Awful Pawful had a claw-full of sock, but it was imprisoned. Chewy Shoes had caught the Awful Pawful before it terrier-ized the dogs of Doggeroo. I was glad, but angry. This was *my* case, not his.

I was about to go home when I saw something else.

Chewy Shoes put his bleeding hand in his pocket and pulled out two little packets. One had fish treats in it.

"Here, kitty, kitty!" Chewy Shoes dangled a fish treat above the cage.

The Awful Pawful yowled. I heard claws *scritttch* the bars of the cage.

"You want this?" said Chewy Shoes.

He opened the other packet. I *sniff-sniffed* a bitter smell.

Chewy Shoes sprinkled some of the

stuff over the fish treats and tossed them at the cage. One piece landed just outside, but most bounced off the Awful Pawful.

"Sleep well, kitty." Chewy Shoes put the packets in his pocket and strolled away.

I stayed put. The Awful Pawful growled, hissed, and cat-erwauled.

Something wasn't right. I felt it in my bones.

How can this be wrong? I asked myself. *A brave person caught the Awful Pawful. Now it can't hurt Doggeroo dogs.*

Suddenly, the Awful Pawful crouched at one end of the cage and stared straight at me. It knew I was there.

It hissed, showing fangs longer than Red's and sharper than Ralf Boxer's.

I buried my nose in my paws. I would have run home, but how could I? I was on a **doggo obbo**, and besides . . .

<u>Jack's Facts</u>

Turning your back on an enemy is a bad idea.
Getting caught by the tail is embarrassing.
This is a fact.

I heard crunching. The monster cat was eating the fish treats. When it had finished, it licked its whiskers and smirked at me. It cat-erwauled and hissed. I think it said something about eating dogs for breakfast.

"If you're so smart, why are you in a cage?" I asked.

The hissing died back to a low mutter. The huge scary eyes closed. The Awful Pawful was asleep.

When I was sure it wasn't pretending, I crept out to investigate. There was a fish treat outside the cage. I hooked it with my paw and subjected it to **jaw-rensic testing**. It tasted bitter, so I spat it out.

Jack's Facts

Good food tastes good.
Bad food sometimes tastes good, too.
If food that should taste good tastes bad,
it probably is bad.
Bad food should be spat out.
This is a fact.

The monster cat snored. I had to do what dogs do . . . but I didn't do it up against a tree. That's when I realized what had happened. Chewy Shoes had **nobbled** the Awful Pawful.

Jack's Glossary

Claw-full. _Paw full of claws, something cats have._

Doggo obbo. _Official observation, performed by a dog._

Jaw-rensic testing. _Testing done by chewing._

Nobbled. _Fed sleepy stuff._

Kitnapped

I don't know how long I stayed on
doggo obbo, watching the Awful Pawful
sleep. I expected Chewy Shoes to fetch
Ranger Jack.

If Sarge was home, I would have
barked for back-up.

Should I consult Foxy? Polly Smote?
Jill Russell? Perhaps I should **interrier-
gate** the squekes? I could fetch Lord Red.
He would ask silly questions. I could
answer them, or make a nose map.

None of this seemed **paw-tinent to
the case**.

Then I had an idea. The Awful

Pawful wasn't going anywhere. I would track Chewy Shoes in case he was seeking Sarge.

Picking up Chewy Shoes' trail was easy, and it felt good to be active.

There were plenty of scents in the preserve. I detected rabbits, Polly Smote, Shuffle the pug, sparrows, and Red. None took my nose off the job for an instant. I was on the track. *Nothing* distracts a tracking Jack.

I mean, almost nothing.

Then I caught a whiff of something that did. Preacher.

Why was the pup here? I had sent him home with Red. At first I was cross. Then I thought of something pawfectly horrible. Chewy Shoes had nobbled the Awful Pawful with fish treats. What if he **doggled** the pup with a liver treat?

I made a quick nose map.

Jack's Map

1. *Awful Pawful.*

2. *Fish Treats.*

3. *Chewy Shoes.*

4. *Foxy.*

5. *Preacher.*

47

"Foxy! Preacher!" I hissed. "Get your paws here on the double. I'm tracking a suspect."

"Is it the yucky person, Dad?" asked Preacher, appearing with Foxy.

I gave him a quick **nose-over**. "Where's Red?"

"A person called Caterina Smith dragged him into a car," said Preacher. "She didn't get me. I hid."

"He was alone," yapped Foxy. "Anyone might have found him!"

"Foxy is looking after me," said Preacher. "He taught me lots of things. I found out how to steal liv—"

"I'll take him home now," said Foxy quickly. "Come, pup. Jack needs to detect."

"Wait!" I told Foxy and Preacher about the Awful Pawful and Chewy Shoes.

Foxy scratched his front elbows with

his hind claws. "Sounds like this Chewy Shoes is a **catsnatcher**," he said. "How does that make him a suspect?" He scratched his ear. "That creature *is* locked up?"

"Of paws," I said. "Chewy Shoes is a **pup-lick benefactor**. Case closed."

Jack's Facts

Thinking something wrong is not right?
You're probably right.
Thinking something wrong is right?
You're probably wrong.
This is a fact.

As we trotted home, I asked Foxy why he had stopped hating Preacher.

Foxy sniffed. "He said you said you trusted me."

We got home just in time to meet

Auntie Tidge coming in my gate. Of paws, we pretended we'd been there all along. I **greeted** her, and knocked her glasses sideways. She loves it when I do that.

"Hello, Foxy Woxy and Jackie Wackie," said Auntie Tidge. "Hello, Preacher Creature." She picked us up and cuddled us all. "I must pop in and water the fern."

She unlocked our front door. Our kitchen seemed empty without Sarge. I missed him all over again. Auntie Tidge is the best cuddler in the world, but she isn't Sarge. This is a *fact*.

"Oh, look at that," said Auntie Tidge, staring at the terrier-phone. I could see a light blinking beside it. "Sarge's new answer machine is working!" She poked about and the light stopped. A woman's voice came out of nowhere.

"Sergeant Russell? Are you there? This is Katya Gibbons. Do you remember my valuable purebred cat, Thumper Bluey? He—er—got loose in Doggeroo once before. Mr. Antikat, my new assistant, says he's disappeared again. I wondered if he might be in Doggeroo? Um . . ." The voice stopped.

"How odd," said Auntie Tidge. "Katya Gibbons . . . I know! Judge Gibbons' wife. She breeds cats."

I tried to **Jack-attack** Auntie Tidge to get her attention. It was no use. Auntie Tidge doesn't wear trousers and you can't Jack-attack bare ankles. I Jack-yapped instead.

"Hungry, Jackie Wackie? Maybe I can find you a liver treat." Auntie Tidge bent to pick me up, and the terrier-phone squawked again. The same voice started talking.

"Sergeant Russell? I just got a ransom demand! Please help me! Someone has **kitnapped** Thumper Bluey! If I don't pay up, he'll cut off Bluey's whiskers and send them in the mail!"

Jack's Glossary

Interrier-gate. *Official questioning, done by a terrier.*

Paw-tinent to the case. *Important to the case.*

Doggled. *Like nobbling a racehorse by doing something that will stop it from winning a race, but done to a dog.*

Nose-over. *Health check carried out by the nose.*

Catsnatcher. *Someone who snatches or kitnaps cats.*

Jack's Glossary

Pup-lick benefactor. *Someone who has just done the dogs of Doggeroo a favor.*

Greet. *This is done by rising to the hind legs and clutching a person with the paws while slurping them up the face.*

Jack-attack. *Growling and biting and pulling at trouser legs. Very loud. Quite harmless.*

Kitnapped. *Same as dognapped, only done to a cat.*

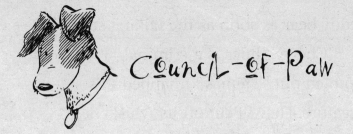

Council-of-Paw

"Oh dear," said Auntie Tidge. "Sarge needs his rest . . . maybe I should ring Inspector Kipper back in the city? Now, what's his number. . . ."

I didn't Jack-attack Auntie Tidge again. She is pawfect for cuddles and treats, but this was a job for a dogged detective.

"Jack Russell's the name, detection's the game," I said.

I slipped out through the dogdoor, and called a **council-of-paw** with Foxy and Preacher. Preacher fell asleep on his teddy bear as soon as the talking started.

"Chewy Shoes is a criminal," I pointed out. "He has kitnapped this creature. He will cut off its whiskers. A cat without whiskers is like a dog without a super-sniffer."

"Do we care?" asked Foxy, scratching. "That creature would bite *your* super-sniffer off if it managed to **cat-ch** you."

This was true. The Awful Pawful was a monster. It would hurt any dog it could cat-ch. Then I thought of something.

"If Chewy Shoes gets away with this, what next? He might dognap Lord Red. Or Preacher. Or you."

Foxy's lip lifted. "Not me. You," growled Foxy.

I knew I could outsmart any dognapper, but I let Foxy think he was

su-paw-rior. "Chewy Shoes must be stopped," I said. "Are you with me?"

"I **sup-paws** so," said Foxy. He looked at Preacher. "Do you really want to free that creature? Do you want it cat-erwauling around Doggeroo, terrier-izing pups and squekes, and making brave dogs hide under beds?"

"No," I said.

"So what are you going to do?" asked Foxy.

"I don't know," I admitted. "I must assess the situation."

"Assess it then," said Foxy. "I'll look after the pup."

I trotted back to the preserve and slunk through the bushes to check on the kitnapped creature. It was still snoring. It still had its whiskers. It didn't

look well. Half a pink tongue was
hanging out and dribbling.

I checked the cage. It was chained
shut. When my super-sniffer detected
Chewy Shoes, I hopped backward and
hid under a bush.

Chewy Shoes kicked the cage. He snarled, like Foxy in a bad mood. He took a pair of clippers out of his pocket, and started unchaining the cage door.

Yeeeowww-wongwongwong!
Psssssssttt!

The Awful Pawful woke up and sprang at Chewy Shoes, who yelled and kicked the cage again, hard.

"Last chance! She pays up, or you're history!"

Chewy Shoes wrapped a bit of cloth around his bleeding hand, and stamped away. The Awful Pawful flopped down. It glared at me, and hissed, but not loudly.

It looked as sick as Sarge when the ambulance took him away.

I didn't offer any help. Cats don't

understand **dogspeak**. Anyway, I still didn't know what to do.

I tracked Chewy Shoes to the Doggeroo Hotel, near Tina Boxer's shop. I **pawtrolled** until it was dark, then trotted home to report to my **second-in-command**.

"So, you didn't get anywhere," said Foxy.

"I tracked the suspect to his lair," I corrected. "I know where he is holed up. I know the method and the motive. I know where he stashed the victim. I'd call that a result, wouldn't you?"

"Not when you can't do anything about it," said Foxy.

"I could if Sarge was here."

"Hi, Dad!" Preacher had been asleep

on his teddy bear. He came over to me and wagged his tail. "Guess what Uncle Foxy and I did."

"Did you play with a ball?" I asked.

Preacher tried to scratch his elbow and fell over. "Uncle Foxy and I went to Ralf Boxer's house. He's smaller than me, but he says he's grown-up. Look what I got on the way home!"

Preacher went back to his bear and scrambled underneath.

"So, what are you going to do?" asked Foxy. "Are you ready to make an arrest? Do you need backup? Maybe we should involve Lord Red. Or—"

Foxy was babbling.

"Dad, look!" Preacher trotted back with a plastic chop in his teeth.

I looked. I sniffed. "Preacher," I said

sternly. "That chop belongs to the squekes. Did you steal it?"

"Of paws!" said Preacher, waggling. "Uncle Foxy says the squekes will yip after it."

"You will take that chop back," I said. "And in the future, *Uncle Foxy* . . ." I glared at Foxy. "Stop teaching the pup to steal!"

Foxy scratched himself. "The squekes will get it back."

I shuddered. There are three squekes. Sometimes that is three too many.

On the other paw, sometimes *one* Foxy is one too many.

I decided not to fuss, in case Foxy got snappy and snarly again. Besides, it had given me a tiny idea.

Jack's Glossary

Council-of-paw. *Council of war, for dogs.*

Cat-ch. *Grab, as a cat does to a mouse.*

Su-paw-rior. *Superior, the way Jack Russells are.*

Sup-paws. *Like suppose, but for dogs.*

Dogspeak. *The private language of dogs.*

Pawtrol. *Patrol, done by a dog.*

Second-in-command. *The one that is almost as smart as the pack leader.*

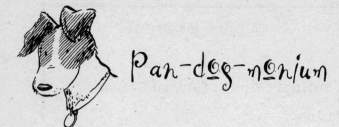

Pan-dog-monium

I went to my basket to think things through.

To catch a human criminal, a dog needs help.

Usually, I would bark for Sarge. I would Jack-attack his leg so he would follow. With Sarge away, there was only one person who could deal with Chewy Shoes *and* the Awful Pawful. Ranger Jack.

How could I get Ranger Jack to the scene of the crime? How could I show him where the criminal was holed up? This called for crafty planning and expert timing.

Just before lunch, Auntie Tidge went

out in a hurry. I told Foxy and Preacher my plan.

"What do you want me to steal?" asked Foxy.

"A chewy shoe. It belongs to the kitnapper who is holed up at the Doggeroo Guest House. Preacher can identify him. When you have eyeballed the suspect, take Preacher to safety. Get the goods and come to the preserve. Nose map the Awful Pawful and bring the shoe to me. Got it?"

"Got it," said Foxy. "Preacher?"

"Got it!" yipped Preacher. "Will I help you solve a case, Dad?"

"You *both* will," I said. "Signal me when you have the evidence."

Foxy and Preacher set off, and after a while I heard a signal from the preserve.

Now came the tricky part. I had to

locate Ranger Jack, and get him to follow
me. I couldn't let him catch me. I
galloped to the showground, where
Preacher and I had sniffed him before.
His van was parked under a tree.

"Go for it, Jack!" I told myself. I
darted up to the van. I bounced around,
yapping and wagging my tail. I pranced
like Lord Red. "Come and get meeeeee!"
I howled.

Ranger Jack was eating lunch. He
popped his head out the van window.
"Jack Russell! Go home!"

I Jack-jumped and flung myself at the
van. I greeted the door, scratching my
claws on the paint.

Ranger Jack leaped out to make a
grab at me. His hat fell off. I grabbed it in
my **Jack-jaws** and took off for the
preserve.

Ranger Jack took off after me. It was as easy as that.

I reached the bushes just as Foxy trotted up, dragging Chewy Shoes' shoe. I danced and pranced around the bushes while Foxy planted the evidence near the cage.

Then I shot under the bushes.

After that, it got noisy. Foxy and I yapped. The Awful Pawful cat-erwauled. Ranger Jack fell over the cage. He yelled, and put his hand out to save himself. And then he *really* yelled.

Foxy and I danced out, barking. Ranger Jack ignored us. He had his hands full with the Awful Pawful. Finally, he backed off and wiped his scratched hand. I retreated under the bushes, but Foxy did what dogs do. He didn't do it against a tree.

Ranger Jack yelled at Foxy.

The Awful Pawful screeched and cat-erwauled and hissed. All this **cat-cophany** attracted Lord Red. Next came Polly Smote, the squekes, Shuffle, Ralf Boxer, and Jill Russell. Of paws they all barked, too. The squekes yipped, demanding their plastic chop. Jill Russell poked me with her nose, demanding Preacher. Ralf Boxer bit Lord Red's toe. Lord Red jumped and howled, and landed on Polly. Polly crawled out from underneath Red and bit Shuffle. Shuffle howled.

Jack's Facts

Ten dogs barking,
plus one kitnapped creature creating
cat-cophany,
plus one ranger yelling,
equals **pan-dog-monium.**
This is a fact.

The case wasn't over yet. Did Ranger Jack have the detective skills to identify the kitnapper?

I was trying to **paw-suade** him to seek the kitnapper when Chewy Shoes came hopping and howling through the bushes. "I'll get you, you *dog*, you!" he yelled. "I'll cut your whiskers off!" He was grabbing at Foxy's tail when he spotted Ranger Jack.

He stared, then yelled. "What are you

doing with my cat?'

Ranger Jack took a huge handful of liver treats out of his pocket and tossed them into the pan-dog-monium. Then he dropped some into the cage with the Awful Pawful.

The cat-cophany and pan-dog-monium stopped. The treat-feasting began.

Ranger Jack pointed at the kitnapper. "Did you throw your shoe at this poor cat?"

Chewy Shoes swiped at Foxy. "That dog stole my shoe, and I came to find it. The cat's mine. The guesthouse wouldn't let me keep it in my room."

Ranger Jack folded his arms. "It's no news to me that some of the local dogs are thieves." He glared at Foxy and me. "However, that cat is not yours. Thumper Bluey belongs to Katya Gibbons. How you came to have him is something you will have to explain to Sergeant Russell."

Chewy Shoes sneered. "He's in the hospital."

"He was," said Ranger Jack. "By now he will be—"

I didn't wait to hear the rest. Sarge was coming home and I *had* to be there to greet him!

Jack's Glossary

Jack-jaws. *The splendid set of jaws owned by a Jack Russell.*

Cat-cophany. *A horrible noise having to do with cats.*

Pan-dog-monium. *A lot of noise that involves dogs.*

Paw-suade. *Persuade, done by a dog.*

Picnic

So, what happened to Chewy Shoes?

His real name was Mr. Antikat. He was Katya Gibbons' assistant. When the Awful Pawful escaped, he tracked it to Doggeroo. Then he kitnapped it to make money. I expect Sarge sent him to the pound.

What about the Awful Pawful?

It rode away in Ranger Jack's van again, Sarge said. Katya Gibbons gave it a secure cat-castle with plenty of chairs to kill.

So, the case of the Kitnapped Creature came to a **successful conclusion**. The Awful Pawful still had its whiskers. The dogs of Doggeroo were safe from its claws. Foxy made friends with Preacher. The kitnapper got sent to the pound. Best of all, Sarge was back where he belonged.

Auntie Tidge and Caterina Smith arranged a river picnic to celebrate. Caterina Smith and Lord Red came. Dora Barkins brought the squekes. The Johnsons came with Gloria Smote, Jill Russell, and Polly. Tina Boxer came with Ralf and Walter Barkly brought Shuffle. Even Kitty Booker came, with Fat Molly in her basket. Foxy, Preacher, and I escorted Sarge and Auntie Tidge. Ranger Jack came, and pretended we were all wearing leashes.

We swam and chased sticks. We dug holes and played hide-and-squeak. Afterward, there were steaks, hot dogs, special biscuits, liver treats, and sausages. It was a pawful lot of fun, especially

when a packet of fish treats went
missing from Kitty Booker's basket.

"*Yooooowwwwfstttt!*" said Molly.

"Dad, are you going to detect the
thief?" Preacher wanted to know.

"No need, pup," I said. "Foxy stole
them."

"I did not!" snapped Foxy. "It was
Preacher."

"It was not!" Preacher leaped up. He
sniff-sniffed Foxy's nose. "It was you,
Uncle Foxy!"

I was pawfully proud of Preacher.

Fat Molly hissed and yowled, and
scared Lord Red.

"Dognappers are after meeeeee!"
howled Red. He leaped up and ran away.

"Lordie, Lorrrdieeeee!" yelled
Caterina Smith.

"We want our chop!" yipped the

squekes. "Preacher, detect our chop!"

"Chop? What chop? I want a chop!" yapped Polly.

"*Now* see what you've done, Jack Russell," said Jill Russell. She poked me with her nose. "You've started another pan-dog-monium!"

I went over to Sarge and settled beside him for a **Jack-nap**. Things were back to normal in Doggeroo.

Jack's Glossary

Successful conclusion. *An ending where everything turns out properly. The criminal is discovered. The kitnapped creature leaves town in a van. The detective is proud of his work. There is plenty to eat.*

Jack-nap. *A well-earned sleep when the detecting is done.*